Scaredy-Pants

A Halloween Story

By Joan Holub
Illustrated by Will Terry

Ready-to-Read • Aladdin
New York London Toronto Sydney

For Kari Scott –J. H.

For Seth and Jackson –W. T.

ALADDIN PAPERBACKS
An imprint of Simon & Schuster Children's Publishing Division
1230 Avenue of the Americas, New York, NY 10020

Designed by Lisa Vega. The text of this book was set in Century Oldstyle BT.
Manufactured in the United States of America.
First Aladdin Paperbacks edition August 2007.
2 4 6 8 10 9 7 5 3 1
Library of Congress Cataloging-in-Publication Data
Holub, Joan.
Scaredy-Pants! / by Joan Holub ; illustrated by Will Terry. — 1st Aladdin Paperbacks ed.
p. cm. — (Ready-to-read) (Ant Hill ; #3)
Summary: While visiting a Halloween fun-house, the ants discover
that not everything is a frightening as it appears to be.
[1. Ants—Fiction. 2. Halloween—Fiction. 3. Haunted houses—Fiction. 4. Fear—Fiction.
5. Stories in rhyme.] I. Terry, Will, 1966- ill. II. Title. III. Title: Ant Hill number three.
PZ8.3.H74Ant 2007   [E]—dc22   2006025717
ISBN-13: 978-1-4169-0956-9 (pbk.)   ISBN-10: 1-4169-0956-7 (pbk.)
ISBN-13: 978-1-4169-2561-3 (lib.)   ISBN-10: 1-4169-2561-9 (lib.)

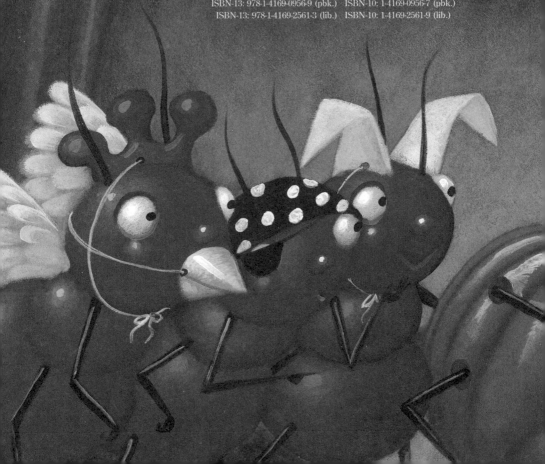

"Go in," said Lynn.
"Who—me?"
asked Dee.

"Afraid?" asked Wade.
"Cluck, cluck," teased Chuck.

"See that?"
asked Matt.

"Not me!"
said Dee.

"A trail!" said Gail.
"Come on," said Dawn.

"Feel that?" asked Matt.

"Not me!" said Dee.

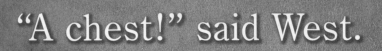
"A chest!" said West.

"A key," said Lee.

"Look in," said Lynn.

"Scaredy-pants!"
said the ants.

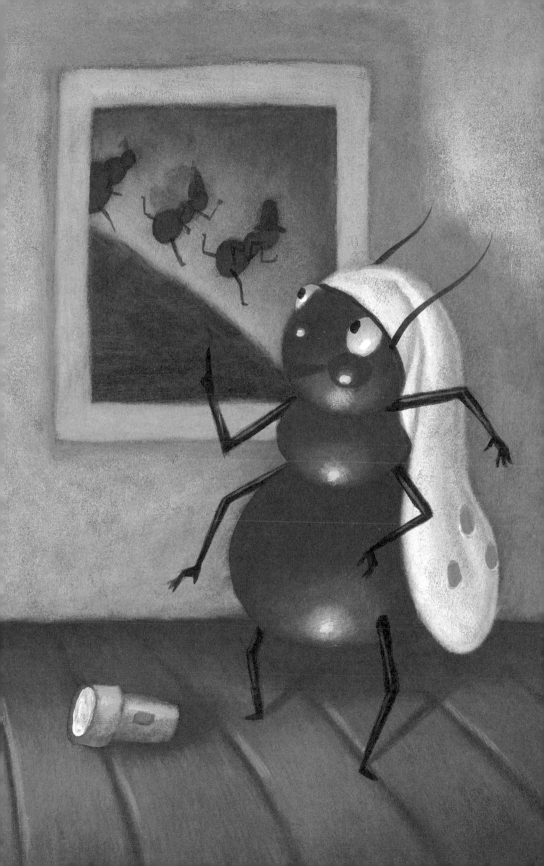